# I'm Revolting

by Gracie Gardner

**FOR PRODUCTION INQUIRIES**

UNITED STATES AND CANADA
info@concordtheatricals.com
1-866-979-0447

UNITED KINGDOM AND EUROPE
licensing@concordtheatricals.co.uk
020-7054-7298

Each title is subject to availability from Concord Theatricals Corp., depending upon country of performance. Please be aware that *I'M REVOLTING* may not be licensed by Concord Theatricals Corp. in your territory. Professional and amateur producers should contact the nearest Concord Theatricals Corp. office or licensing partner to verify availability.

No one shall make any changes in this title(s) for the purpose of production. No part of this book may be reproduced, stored in a retrieval system, scanned, uploaded, or transmitted in any form, by any means, now known or yet to be invented, including mechanical, electronic, digital, photocopying, recording, videotaping, or otherwise, without the prior written permission of the publisher. No one shall share this title(s), or any part of this title(s), through any social media or file hosting websites.

For all inquiries regarding motion picture, television, online/digital and other media rights, please contact Concord Theatricals Corp.

## MUSIC AND THIRD-PARTY MATERIALS USE NOTE

Licensees are solely responsible for obtaining formal written permission from copyright owners to use copyrighted music and/or other copyrighted third-party materials (e.g. artworks, logos) in the performance of this play and are strongly cautioned to do so. If no such permission is obtained by the licensee, then the licensee must use only original music and materials that the licensee owns and controls. Licensees are solely responsible and liable for clearances of all third-party copyrighted materials, including without limitation music, and shall indemnify the copyright owners of the play(s) and their licensing agent, Concord Theatricals Corp., against any costs, expenses, losses and liabilities arising from the use of such copyrighted third-party materials by licensees. For music, please contact the appropriate music licensing authority in your territory for the rights to any incidental music.

## IMPORTANT BILLING AND CREDIT REQUIREMENTS

If you have obtained performance rights to this title, please refer to your licensing agreement for important billing and credit requirements.

*I'M REVOLTING* was first produced by the Atlantic Theater Company in New York City on September 8, 2022. The performance was directed by Knud Adams, with sets by Marsha Ginsberg, costumes by Enver Chakartash, lighting design by Kate McGee, sound design by Bray Poor, and hair and makeup design by Caroline Schettler. The Production Stage Manager was Alex H. Hajjar. The cast was as follows:

**JONATHAN** . . . . . . . . . . . . . . . . . . . . . . . . . . . . . . . . . . . . . Bartley Booz

**DENISE** . . . . . . . . . . . . . . . . . . . . . . . . . . . . . Patrice Johnson Chavannes

**REGGIE** . . . . . . . . . . . . . . . . . . . . . . . . . . . . . . . . . . . Alicia Pilgrim

**ANNA** . . . . . . . . . . . . . . . . . . . . . . . . . . . . . . . . . . . . . . . Gabby Beans

**LIANE** . . . . . . . . . . . . . . . . . . . . . . . . . . . . . . . Emily Cass McDonnell

**JORDAN** . . . . . . . . . . . . . . . . . . . . . . . . . . . . . . . . . . Glenn Fitzgerald

**CLYDE** . . . . . . . . . . . . . . . . . . . . . . . . . . . . . . . . . . . . . Peter Gerety

**TOBY** . . . . . . . . . . . . . . . . . . . . . . . . . . . . . . . . . . . . . . Patrick Vaill

**PAULA** . . . . . . . . . . . . . . . . . . . . . . . . . . . . . . . . . . . Laura Esterman

# CHARACTERS

**JONATHAN** – M, 29
**DENISE** – F, 62
**REGGIE** – F, 19
**ANNA** – F, 26
**LIANE** – F, 56
**JORDAN** – M, 57
**CLYDE** – M, 78
**TOBY** – M, 49
**PAULA** – F, 76

*To my parents.*

# (8 A.M.)

*(December, 2019, New York. A waiting room. A vending machine. A hallway leading to an offstage surgical suite. There's a cardboard cutout of a woman holding a sign that says: "ALDARA (IMIQUIMOD) IS NOW FDA APPROVED! NO SURGERY NEEDED! ASK YOUR DOCTOR TODAY.")*

*(**DENISE** walks in, bundled up, looking at her phone, removing a glove with her teeth to type a text, glove dangling from her mouth. **JONATHAN** walks on with a laptop, frazzled.)*

**JONATHAN.** Uh, the float nurse isn't here... Doctor James?

**DENISE.** *(Still typing.)* The float request was. Denied.

*(The text shoots off.)*

**JONATHAN.** I could steal a nurse from upstairs?

**DENISE.** What do you mean steal. A nurse.

**JONATHAN.** I...don't. Know.

**DENISE.** *(Getting ready.)* Let's go over the day.

**JONATHAN.** First up! Nineteen-year-old female, basal cell, nasal tip, two centimeters, looks like she's taken Isotretinoin for...a thousand years.

**DENISE.** How many years?

**JONATHAN.** Um, four. And, so, she's very young. Do you want to get a social worker involved?

**DENISE.**  I'll observe, what do you want to do?

**JONATHAN.**  Depends how bad it is?

**DENISE.**  If we do a flap I'd call psych for a consult.

**JONATHAN.**  Understood. Next: forty-year-old male, lentigo maligna, left nipple, um, depression, runs tachy, Bupropion, Alprazolam, referred from Penn, noncompliant.

**DENISE.**  I'll observe.

**JONATHAN.**  You do have a peer-to-peer with Aetna at nine.

**DENISE.**  Never mind! You're on your own.

**JONATHAN.**  On my what?

**DENISE.**  Scrape it, plate it, date it.

**JONATHAN.**  It's just a pre-auth. Can't you reschedule?

**DENISE.**  No. We deal with it, and move on. What's next?

**JONATHAN.**  Seventy-year-old male, squamous cell, neck, looks like he's a frequent flyer? Clyde?

**DENISE.**  Clyde. We love Clyde.

**JONATHAN.**  Do you need clinicals?

**DENISE.**  Just updates.

**JONATHAN.**  I do see Patty noted he just retired. And diabetes mellitus, glyburide, insulin.

**DENISE.**  That sucks. You'll observe. He's...not gonna like your vibe.

**JONATHAN.**  We'll see about that! Um, and last up, forty-five-year-old female, referral from a Dr. Paige in Toledo.

**DENISE.**  Right.

**JONATHAN.**  Invasive complex sarcoma, medial canthus, nasal bridge, she's done four rounds of local radiation, topical chemo, is this right, five centimeters?

**DENISE.** Is that what it says?

**JONATHAN.** Yeah.

**DENISE.** Gross! That's gonna be horrible. We'll see what's there but... Sounds like enucleation.

**JONATHAN.** I've never actually observed one before.

**DENISE.** Observe? You can hold the spoon!

**JONATHAN.** Alright! Question: you have consults scheduled upstairs from noon to one. Can I come with you for that?

**DENISE.** No, I need you to run path.

**JONATHAN.** That's fair.

*(She clocks the cutout.)*

**DENISE.** Is this what they sent?

**JONATHAN.** I know, I thought it would be more discreet. And then following passes? Um, how long do you expect that will take?

**DENISE.** And what do you mean?

**JONATHAN.** I just, I don't know if last week was...normal. I guess I thought derm had, better, um. Hours. I have tickets.

**DENISE.** You made *plans*?

**JONATHAN.** I...did? I did.

**DENISE.** Don't do that.

*(**REGGIE** enters.)*

**REGGIE.** Am I in the right place? I have like, skin cancer?

**JONATHAN.** Regina?

**REGGIE.** Reggie.

**DENISE.** Denise. We keep it cajzh here. I'll be your attending. And Jonathan will perform your procedure under my supervision.

**REGGIE.**  Hey.

**JONATHAN.**  *(Solemnly.)* What's up.

**REGGIE.**  *(Calmly.)* I'm having a panic attack.

**DENISE.**  That's okay, we can give you something for that.

**REGGIE.**  I looked up this surgery on the internet on the way here.

**DENISE.**  It's not a good idea to look at those images.

**REGGIE.**  It looks like a giant hole in someone's face. Like a big red hole.

**DENISE.**  You're not going to look like that forever.

**REGGIE.**  And I'm gonna be awake the whole time?

**DENISE.**  But you won't feel anything. You'll be all numbed up.

**REGGIE.**  Why do I have to be awake?

**DENISE.**  It's safer this way.

**REGGIE.**  But you said you can give me something?

**DENISE.**  Sure, we can give you beta blockers when you come into the room, but they won't put you to sleep.

**REGGIE.**  So...I'm awake... And...

**DENISE.**  We'll cut around the area where you had the biopsy.

(**DENISE** *looks at* **REGGIE***'s nose under her dermatoscope.*)

Great oil glands, then you'll come out here and wait while the lab takes a look at the margins. Do you have any questions?

**REGGIE.**  Am I gonna have a big scar?

**DENISE.**  You will have *a* scar. Any time we cut, the healing forms scar tissue.

**REGGIE.**  It's gonna look really bad?

**DENISE.** It will look different.

**REGGIE.** Like am I gonna have a nose at all? I'm picturing Voldemort.

**JONATHAN.** *(Serious.)* We'll cross that bridge.

**DENISE.** If the surgery dramatically changes the structure of your face we have ways to ease that transition. We can have a conversation about reconstruction. You can think about a prosthesis or talking to a psychiatrist.

**REGGIE.** Why would I do that?

**DENISE.** Some patients experience an adjustment period. There's a chance you won't totally recognize yourself in the mirror. That can be psychologically disorienting.

**REGGIE.** I can use gels? Lasers? That make the scar go away?

**DENISE.** And what are you thinking of?

**REGGIE.** I've seen commercials.

**DENISE.** You can do whatever you're interested in spending your time and money on.

**REGGIE.** It's not legit?

**DENISE.** It can't hurt. :)

**JONATHAN.** It's mostly time. The gels and lasers all say, "This takes time." It's the tincture of time that heals.

**DENISE.** It's the *body* that heals, and the body takes time.

**REGGIE.** *(Looking at the cutout.)* What about that? Is there any way I could just not do surgery? And do that instead?

**DENISE.** You don't have the right kind of cancer.

### (9 A.M.)

(**TOBY** *is here now, trying to sleep under his parka.* **REGGIE** *now has a bandage over her nose. Her sister* **ANNA** *arrives.*)

**ANNA**. OH MY GOD, your face! That looks so owchies! Oh no, Little Tiny Squishy One! The Smallest Baby One!

**REGGIE**. You are so late!

**ANNA**. I'm sorry, / I'm sorry!

**REGGIE**. I said eight o'clock!

**ANNA**. Do you want me to just leave?

**REGGIE**. Can I criticize you without you threatening to abandon me?

**ANNA**. I've been working since five.

**REGGIE**. The exchange doesn't open 'til nine thirty.

**ANNA**. You think I only work the hours the exchange is open?

**REGGIE**. I'm not impressed that you have no work/life boundary, Anna, I'm feeling scared and alone!

**ANNA**. Call Dad!

**REGGIE**. He doesn't want to see my gay ass!

**ANNA**. You guys *have* to get *over it.*

**REGGIE**. I don't have to do anything!

**ANNA**. If I get married and you two are still fighting on my wedding day? That's gonna be, frankly, incredibly rude to me.

**REGGIE**. We're not "fighting."

**ANNA**. Why don't you just lie to him?

**REGGIE**. Are you serious?

**ANNA.**  He was doing a good job lying to himself already. I mean you spent your entire adolescence in the basement watching *Sailor Moon* and masturbating under that cow blanket. He's in denial.

**REGGIE.**  I really don't think he knew.

**ANNA.**  I mean what did you think he was gonna say when you came out?

**REGGIE.**  "You're my daughter, and I love you."

**ANNA.**  That's so deranged that you thought he would say that!

(**ANNA***'s on her AirPods.*)

Sophie I'm not in yet. No. No. He can't. That's not my purview. Not my purview. Not my purview. Your last boss said that? Yeah well he's in jail now so I'm hanging up.

(**ANNA** *huffs.*)

Um, you look like a *bird.*

**REGGIE.**  I look like Jack Nicholson in *Chinatown.*

**ANNA.**  I don't know what that means.

**REGGIE.**  It's a classic.

**ANNA.**  Don't be pretentious. Does it hurt?

**REGGIE.**  I'm still numb.

**ANNA.**  How much longer do you have to stay?

**REGGIE.**  I don't know.

**ANNA.**  Do you think you can leave in the next fifteen, twenty minutes?

**REGGIE.**  No!? It could take all day.

**ANNA.**  *Really?...* I have to go soon.

**REGGIE.**  Anna I explained this to you! You didn't get the day off?

**ANNA.**  *Why does it take so long?*

**REGGIE.**  *I don't know.*

**ANNA.**  How did you even get this??

**REGGIE.**  *I DON'T KNOW!*

**ANNA.**  But it's not the serious kind, right?

**REGGIE.**  No. It's not the serious kind.

**ANNA.**  So you're okay with me leaving you here?

**REGGIE.**  It's on the middle of my face, Anna! Are you kidding me??

**ANNA.**  Reggie, I can't be late for work or I'm gonna get fired.

**REGGIE.**  Then don't be late for work!

**ANNA.**  *(Bad Italian accent.)* But I wahnt to be here for my seester.

**REGGIE.**  If you're just going to sit here and stress about work that's not really "being here" for me.

**ANNA.**  I know you don't totally understand my job, but analysts *do not* take days off.

**REGGIE.**  Okay.

**ANNA.**  Like, that is unheard of. I went in when I had giardia. I kept plastic bags in my bra! Barf, toss, I kept *going.*

**REGGIE.**  Gross.

**ANNA.**  *(An offering.)* I brought you yummies!

(**ANNA** *presents a sad Quest bar.*)

---

*A license to produce *I'm Revolting* does not include a license to publicly display any branded logos or trademarked images. Licensees must acquire rights for any logos and/or images or create their own.

**REGGIE.** Was this just… In your bag?

**ANNA.** *(It was.)* No!

(**REGGIE** *looks at the nutritional information.*)

**REGGIE.** There's whey in this.

**ANNA.** Are you vegan *again*? Reggie. I can't keep up. I'm *exhausted*.

(**REGGIE** *eats the bar.*)

**REGGIE.** This tastes like…the inside of your bag. How long has it been in there?

(**ANNA** *becomes abruptly immersed in her phone.*)

What's going on?

**ANNA.** What if I told work: "My little sister has cancer."

**REGGIE.** I mean it's technically true. But I feel like I have to say, "Oh it's just a little thing." Like I didn't tell anyone I had "cancer."

**ANNA.** My sister has *"just a little thing"* ?? *That's not gonna work.*

**REGGIE.** I don't feel like it's a serious enough cancer to say it's cancer.

(**JORDAN** *and* **LIANE** *come on.* **JORDAN** *wears a carpal tunnel brace on his wrist.* **LIANE** *has some bandages on her face.*)

**LIANE.** You *really* didn't bring the cream?

**JORDAN.** It's a little late for that, don't you think?

**LIANE.** I asked you to bring the big one because I wanted to use it today.

**JORDAN.** Why would you tell me to do that when it takes the time to tell me to just do it yourself?

**LIANE.**  Maybe the nurse has some.

>         (**LIANE** *puts her pocketbook down and goes
>         off.* **ANNA** *makes a "yikes" face.*)

**ANNA.**  You have *nothing* to worry about, did you see that?

**REGGIE.**  SHHHH!!

**ANNA.**  Where are my plastic bags?

**REGGIE.**  You're turning into Dad and it's honestly terrifying. *No* self awareness.

**ANNA.**  You don't know these people.

>         (**REGGIE** *is trying to zen out.*)

**REGGIE.**  The drugs they gave me suck. I feel completely normal.

**ANNA.**  What did they give you?

**REGGIE.**  Beta blockers?

**ANNA.**  Beta blockers don't get you high, Reggie.

**REGGIE.**  God damnit!

**ANNA.**  What even is this place? Why aren't you at the famous place?

**REGGIE.**  !!! I don't know how to find a doctor! I just Googled, "best" and none of those were in my network!

**ANNA.**  Well good, those "Top Doctor" lists are payola. You're still on dad's insurance?

**REGGIE.**  Yeah.

**ANNA.**  And this is covered?

**REGGIE.**  That's what they told me. But when I had to get my contacts renewed I got a bill for seven hundred dollars for an eye exam. And they said that was covered. How is that legal?

**ANNA.** Supplier induced demand.

**REGGIE.** What does that mean?

**ANNA.** They can do whatever they want.

**REGGIE.** How do *you* find a doctor?

**ANNA.** Um, I ask a super rich person what doctor they go to.

**REGGIE.** That's what I did, I asked my roommate. She said her mom went here.

**ANNA.** Who's your roommate?

**REGGIE.** Danielle?

**ANNA.** Where's she from?

**REGGIE.** Manhattan Valley.

**ANNA.** Where'd she go to high school?

**REGGIE.** Dalton.

**ANNA.** Does she wear a strap on her sunglasses?

**REGGIE.** Uh...? Yeah...?

**ANNA.** *(Considering, nodding.)* ...Good. That means she has a boat. What did it look like?

**REGGIE.** I mean I had a zit there for a long time. Or, I thought it was a zit.

**ANNA.** *(Fondly recalling.)* Oh yeah! You did! It was like a perma-zit.

**REGGIE.** Y...Yep.

**ANNA.** Okay.

**REGGIE.** I tried everything to get rid of it. I did the Ordinary. I did the Aesop cream. I did retinol. But it kept getting angrier. And then I got desperate and bought this laser treatment off Groupon.

(**ANNA** *gasps.*)

**ANNA**.  NO!

**REGGIE**.  And it...it... Fell off.

> (**ANNA** *gasps.*)

**ANNA**.  Oh my goddddddd.

**REGGIE**.  So I saw this dermatologist who thought it was nothing. So I went to a plastic surgeon to be like, *please* take this weird thing off my face and he took one look at it and was like, yeah, that's fucked, I'm sending it to a lab.

**ANNA**.  Well good! You got a second opinion.

**REGGIE**.  I don't understand how a *dermatologist* doesn't know what skin cancer looks like. That really freaked me out.

**ANNA**.  Um, med school is pass/fail.

**REGGIE**.  Like gym class?

**ANNA**.  Yeah, you need to do your research. Did you research this place?

**REGGIE**.  Yes! I did, Anna!

**ANNA**.  It's your *face*.

**REGGIE**.  I know!

**ANNA**.  Did you check if this doctor gets kickbacks?

**REGGIE**.  What?

**ANNA**.  From pharma companies?

**REGGIE**.  I don't even know what you're talking about.

**ANNA**.  You can see how much money they get for prescribing stuff!

**REGGIE**.  She's not prescribing me anything... They're literally removing the cancer with their hands. Please stop looking for ways to be condescending and just... Do the thing you're supposed to do in this situation!

(**ANNA** *thinks about what she's supposed to do. She awkwardly pats* **REGGIE**'s *shoulder in a mock gesture of care.* **REGGIE** *glowers at her.* **JONATHAN** *enters with a tablet.*)

**JONATHAN.** Reggie?

**ANNA.** Can she go?

**JONATHAN.** This is your?

**ANNA.** Healthcare Proxy.     **REGGIE.** Sister.

**JONATHAN.** We're going to have you stay a little bit longer.

**ANNA.** I have to go? And I'd like to take her home before then. Is there anything I can do to speed this up?

(**ANNA** *casually folds her arms, a hundred dollar bill in her fingers.* **JONATHAN** *clocks the bill.*)

**JONATHAN.** Unfortunately it just takes the time it takes. She could be here for another couple hours or until this evening. I just have some forms for you to sign. Standard acknowledgement of risk. Loss of sensation. Facial mobility. Droopy eyelid. Sense of smell. There's a few more.

**ANNA.** That's a real thing? *Droopy eyelid?*

**JONATHAN.** It...is? It is.

**ANNA.** Shouldn't she have signed this before you started?

**JONATHAN.** We're a little short-staffed at the moment.

**ANNA.** (*Studying him.*) ...Are you a real doctor?

**JONATHAN.** Ha ha. Yes.

**ANNA.** You look *quite fresh.*

**JONATHAN.** I am a resident.

**ANNA.** So you're just out of school?

**JONATHAN.** No, I've completed med school, and an internship. I'm a physician.

**ANNA.** And when did you finish this internship?

**REGGIE.** He's not my main doctor!

**ANNA.** Who is holding the scalpel?

**REGGIE.** Well, he is.

**ANNA.** Where did you go to medical school?

**JONATHAN.** Geisel... It's... (It's Dartmouth.)

**ANNA.** I don't want to talk to you? Again. I want to speak to the attending. May I read this?

**JONATHAN.** Of course! Let me know if you have any questions.

        (**JONATHAN** *goes.*)

**ANNA.** *Dartmouth! Has a beer keg! For a mascot!*

**REGGIE.** It's an Ivy!

**ANNA.** I don't agree with that! DO NOT let Doogie Howser touch your face. You *insist* on the attending, okay?

**REGGIE.** I didn't know you could do that.

**ANNA.** People say there are rules? But there are no rules. If something seems wrong...advocate for yourself. Do you think you can do that?

**REGGIE.** ...Yeah.

        (**REGGIE** *starts signing the forms.*)

**ANNA.** Read it first!

**REGGIE.** Okay...!

**ANNA.** You have no idea what you are signing away in waivers every day. Your data is being used and sold / for profit because, you know, you want validation.

**REGGIE.** Can I read / this?

**ANNA.** Yes! Yes.

*(Pause.)*

*(Grumbling.)* Like Mimi always posts pictures of her kids online?

I just think it's unethical to capitalize on your children for social currency.

**REGGIE.** *(Without looking up.)* Her kids are cute, I like seeing them grow up.

**ANNA.** Then you are complicit in the game, they will never have the option of anonymity they deserve because you demand the marketplace.

**REGGIE.** Why is it every time I have to do something important, like study for the SATs, you get in my face and bring up, like, the Israeli-Palestinian Conflict?!

**ANNA.** I'm sorry.

*(She's not gonna bring it up. She's not. She's not! And then:)*

It's Britain's fault.

**REGGIE.** Annnn*nnnna!*

**ANNA.** They shouldn't have promised the land to both of them!

**(JONATHAN** *returns for the tablet.)*

*(At* **JONATHAN.***)* NO!...NO.

**(JONATHAN** *goes back inside.)*

**REGGIE.** Anna! Please don't be rude to this man! He's got sharpened implements close to my beautiful face!

**ANNA.**  What if he did it wrong, and then they're like… "We got it all." But there's actually more that they can't see, the borders are undefined, and they try to put it back together, like…

**REGGIE.**  Don't…

**ANNA.**  Israel… What then?

**REGGIE.**  I am not going to participate in this analogy!

**ANNA.**  Hi Andy!

>   (**ANNA**'s *picked up a call on her AirPods.*)

>   (*Andy's on the exchange floor.*)

I was just about to call you –

>   (**TOBY** *huffs under his parka.* **ANNA** *gives* **REGGIE** *the "just one sec" finger.*)

(*Exiting.*) Yeah, so actually…My sister has CANCER. So…

>   (**LIANE** *enters.*)

**LIANE.**  There's no nurse here. A little doctor guy gave it to me.

**JORDAN.**  It doesn't do any good.

**LIANE.**  The cream?

**JORDAN.**  We're *here.* Aren't we kind of past this?

**LIANE.**  It's supposed to shrink it down.

**JORDAN.**  It's not gonna do anything twenty minutes before you go in.

**LIANE.**  I'm just following what Dr. Paige said to do.

**JORDAN.**  Okay… *Now* you're following what your doctor told you to do.

**LIANE.**  Jesus, Jordan.

**JORDAN.** Patient outcome...is patient compliance...

**LIANE.** *Jordan.*

**JORDAN.** And it's so frustrating, to be here now, when I've spent two decades going to the / office to do patient compliance.

**LIANE.** You throw out your Z-Paks on day three.

**JORDAN.** That / is not the same!

**LIANE.** You get exactly as better as you need to be / and then to hell with it.

**JORDAN.** This is my life's work? So. This is what I've worked on every day.

**LIANE.** I'm sorry your mother told you you'd be good at that.

**JORDAN.** You *cannot* bring up my mother in this moment.

**LIANE.** I certainly don't want to think about your mother in this moment. I don't want to think about your mother *at all.*

**JORDAN.** Should we call her? / Should I get her on the phone right now? For support?

**LIANE.** Is that what you want? Do you wanna call her? Jordan? Maybe you need her support for this very hard thing *you're* going through.

> (**JORDAN** *suspends his hand in the air, grasping for the impossible mother his mother never was and his wife will never be.*)

**JORDAN.** My mother –

> (**TOBY** *moans.*)

If she were here right now...

**LIANE.** What would she be doing in this moment? She's here now. What is she doing, Jordan?

**JORDAN**. She's listening to me, and she's hearing me.

**LIANE**. She's listening to you. Ohhhh. That's what she's doing when we're at Car / raba's.

**JORDAN**. Okay.

<table>
<tr><td>LIANE.</td><td>JORDAN. (Continued.)</td></tr>
<tr><td>And she calls you up, and you take the call, and you complain about me to your mother, in front of Jen and Aura. And I'm just livin' in it, sucking down some gluey carbonara.</td><td>I needed support, Liane. You weren't giving me support! I need some empathy. I cannot work. Due to injury. I wasn't complaining! I was telling her the facts of our mutual lives!</td></tr>
</table>

**JORDAN**. *(Continued.)* Is that what we're doing? Just… shitting on the traditions we've set up as a family?

**LIANE**. We don't have a family, Jordan, it's just us, it's just us, / it's just us.

**JORDAN**. Can we talk about this later?

**LIANE**. I don't know, Jordan, are you gonna help me?

> *(She holds out the cream.* **JORDAN** *takes it, peels away at her bandage and starts massaging it into* **LIANE**'s *lesion.* **ANNA** *returns.)*

**ANNA**. I *do* have to go into work.

**REGGIE**. What happened?

**ANNA**. *I tried.*

**REGGIE**. What did he say?

**ANNA**. He said he wouldn't care if I had cancer.

**REGGIE**. What is wrong with him?!

**ANNA**. Pain! The pain that comes from not having enough obstacles in life and needing to create them.

**REGGIE.**  Can you complain about him to management?

**ANNA.**  No, sadomasochism kind of *is* Morgan Stanley's corporate culture.

**REGGIE.**  Okay, well.

**ANNA.**  You'll be out of here in like twelve minutes.

**REGGIE.**  Will you come back if I'm not?

**ANNA.**  Call Dad!

**REGGIE.**  Annnn*nnnna*. I can't. I can't. Please come back? ...Please?

**ANNA.**  Can you keep me in the loop?

## (11 A.M.)

(**REGGIE** *has a larger bandage on her nose.* **LIANE** *is gone,* **JORDAN** *waits for her in his chair.* **TOBY** *is also gone, his stuff keeps his spot.* **CLYDE** *is here now. He is at the vending machine buying sunflower seeds. He goes to his chair, checks the scores, eats the sunflower seeds, and the shells go right on the floor.*)

**CLYDE.** They're up by six.

**JORDAN.** Mm.

**CLYDE.** Can't stay up for that long.

**JORDAN.** Mm hmm.

**CLYDE.** Want some?

**JORDAN.** Oh, no thanks.

(**CLYDE** *shakes the sunflower seeds at* **REGGIE.** **REGGIE** *forces a polite smile and blinks. He shakes the bag again and she smiles and shakes her head.*)

**CLYDE.** They're good for ya! Good for the mitochondria.

**REGGIE.** I don't know how to eat those.

**CLYDE.** What's that?

**REGGIE.** I would have no idea what to do with a sunflower seed.

**CLYDE.** You just eat it. Spit out the shell.

(**REGGIE** *daintily takes a few seeds and tries them.*)

Quite a beak you got there. I had one right there myself.

**REGGIE.** Basal cell?

**CLYDE.** Squamous!

(*Looking at his scar.*)

**REGGIE.** How big was it?

**CLYDE.** Itty bitty.

**REGGIE.** Really? It's, sorry but, kind of a large scar.

**CLYDE.** That's what happens. They start digging, but these things are like icebergs. They don't know how deep it goes until they get in there.

**REGGIE.** How many have you had?

**CLYDE.** Oh this is my yearly pilgrimage.

**REGGIE.** You come here every year?

**CLYDE.** Oh yeah.

**REGGIE.** This is a huge deal for me, and you just...

**CLYDE.** It's routine. Can't let 'em get too big. How'd your wife let that happen?

**REGGIE.** Um!

**JORDAN.** That is a great question.

**CLYDE.** I always wonder when I see someone that bad. You know? What was goin' on there...

**JORDAN.** I'd let Liane tell it...

**CLYDE.** Didn't you notice it? Getting worse?

**JORDAN.** ... ...I didn't. It happened so slowly. I see her every day. And then... Something was so clearly wrong.

**CLYDE.** Me, I know I got one every year.

**JORDAN.** How's that?

**CLYDE.** Each one you get, the chance of you getting another one exponentially rises.

**JORDAN.** Is that so?

**CLYDE.**  Like pulling out gray hairs.

**REGGIE.**  That's a myth.

(**CLYDE** *and* **JORDAN** *look at her.*)

Pulling out gray hair doesn't increase your likelihood of getting gray hair. Pulling out gray hair's like Whack-A-Mole. It's not like cancer. Cancer's like *The Thing*.

**JORDAN.**  *The Thing*.

**REGGIE.**  The movie.

**CLYDE.**  Well I hope she comes out of it okay. Most people come out of there a little dinged up, but some people… You know. It's a bummer.

(**JORDAN** *looks at him.*)

Didn't they say that?

**JORDAN.**  No they did, but, they said a lot of unlikely things.

**CLYDE.**  Oh yeah. They have to cover their asses. Denise doesn't like that I pull out my own stitches.

**REGGIE.**  You can do that?

**CLYDE.**  I'm not driving down here to do something I can accomplish with a pair of fingernail clippers.

**JORDAN.**  Should leave that to the professionals.

**CLYDE.**  Eh.

**REGGIE.**  Where is yours?

**CLYDE.**  Huh?

**REGGIE.**  Where's your cancer?

**CLYDE.**  M'neck.

(**REGGIE** *nods, her leg bounces.*)

You nervous? Don't be nervous. Scars give a person character.

(**CLYDE** *gets a sunflower seed stuck in his throat, coughs, there's a moment where* **JORDAN** *and* **REGGIE** *look at one another. Then,* **CLYDE** *coughs it up.*)

Whew.

(**CLYDE** *returns to his seeds.* **TOBY** *comes back without a bandage, sits down.* **CLYDE** *eyes him.*)

Hey, man. Where's your wound?

**REGGIE.** *(Refereeing* **CLYDE**.*)* Oh, / you know what.

**TOBY.** We really don't have to make small talk.

**CLYDE.** No use in being coy. We're here all day! You have anyone coming?

**TOBY.** My mother is dropping by.

**CLYDE.** That's nice.

**TOBY.** You're here alone?

**CLYDE.** I don't need any uh. Emotional support person. Haha. Emotional support bunny rabbit or…ah… Snake. Ha ha. "I need my snake or I'll freak out."… You're not from the city.

**TOBY.** No I am. I just live in Philly.

**CLYDE.** What do you have?

**TOBY.** Lentigo maligna?

**CLYDE.** *What is that?*

**TOBY.** I don't even know. It's nothing. It's like a weird mole that could become melanoma in theory. I was a lifeguard. Never wore sunscreen. It's my own fault.

**CLYDE.** No, no it's not.

**TOBY.** No I actually feel empowered? When I blame myself? So, it's okay.

**CLYDE.**  Melanoma's not so much from sun. Just bad luck.

**TOBY.**  Oh, well! I'm sure it's a punishment for something else I did wrong.

>(**JONATHAN** *enters.*)

**JONATHAN.**  Clyde? We're ready for you.

**CLYDE.**  Okayyy.

**JONATHAN.**  *(Earnest.)* And um, happy retirement!

**CLYDE.**  What? Who the hell are you?

>(**CLYDE** *follows* **JONATHAN** *down the hallway.* **REGGIE** *turns to* **TOBY**.)

**REGGIE.**  Melanoma. That's really scary.

**TOBY.**  But it's *not* melanoma.

**REGGIE.**  Cancer's cancer.

**TOBY.**  It's not even cancer!

**REGGIE.**  It's not?

**TOBY.**  No. I mean, not yet. Right now it's just a weird mole in a shitty location.

>(**LIANE** *enters, one of her eyes is bandaged.* **JONATHAN** *is helping her walk.*)

**JONATHAN.**  We gave her a sedative, I need you to keep her up. Okay?

**LIANE.**  I'm going home goodbye.

**JONATHAN.**  Liane, you have to stay. We need to make sure we got everything.

**JORDAN.**  I thought you said you weren't gonna sedate her.

**JONATHAN.**  We don't normally, in this case we had to.

**JORDAN.**  What sedative?

**JONATHAN**.  Ketamine.

> (**REGGIE** *perks up.*)

**JORDAN**.  Is that something you give out? I'm not doing so great. Do you…?

**JONATHAN**.  I'm sorry.

> (**JONATHAN** *goes.*)

**LIANE**.  I am my mouth. My teeth are a cage. My tongue will never be free. Will never be dry.

> (*She puts her head between her legs.*)

**JORDAN**.  You need to stay up, Liane. Up up.

**LIANE**.  I'm so embarrassed the GoFundMe FAILED.

**JORDAN**.  Liane.

**LIANE**.  I hated asking, emailing everyone. I'm not a sweetie. People weren't gonna give enough money for me to go to Sloan Kettering.

**JORDAN**.  Liane.

**LIANE**.  I guess if you're kind of a bitch then you have to go to the shitty hospital!

**JORDAN**.  Shhh shhh. It's not a bad hospital!

**LIANE**.  THREE stars on Yelp.

> (**REGGIE** *and* **TOBY** *connect visually and both pull out their phones to check.*)

**JORDAN**.  You don't Yelp a hospital…

**LIANE**.  We should have defaulted. The lawyer who said we should file?

**JORDAN**.  Once you come around to the idea of suing the doctor in Toledo for malpractice.

**LIANE**. No.

**JORDAN**. We'll get a settlement.

**LIANE**. Nonne.

**JORDAN**. And we will be fine.

**LIANE**. YOU are an ambulance chaser.

**JORDAN**. I'm just trying to get you the best care.

**LIANE**. I am not you. I am my mouth. My teeth are a cage. My tongue will never be free. Will never be dry.

**JORDAN**. *What is that?*

**LIANE**. It's THE TRUTH!

> (**LIANE** *drifts off.* **JORDAN** *makes sure she's settled in her chair, grabs a pack of Camels*<sup></sup> from his jacket pocket, gets up and goes out.* **REGGIE** *looks at* **TOBY**.)

**REGGIE**. Are you reading these?

**TOBY**. Yes I am.

**REGGIE**. Do you see the one with – / "This is a place to go and die."

**TOBY**. "This is a place to go and die."

**REGGIE**. I mean it's a cancer facility?

**TOBY**. That review is for upstairs, though, right?

**REGGIE**. Right.

**TOBY**. "Professional and courteous."

**REGGIE**. "Hate my scar."

**TOBY**. "Denise is amazing."

---

* A license to produce *I'm Revolting* does not include a license to publicly display any branded logos or trademarked images. Licensees must acquire rights for any logos and/or images or create their own.

**REGGIE.** "They destroyed my face."

**TOBY.** ...It sort of...shakes out.

**REGGIE.** What is Sloan's like?

**TOBY.** Uh... Oh. Hm. Also three stars. "None of these doctors give a shit."

**REGGIE.** Oh.

**TOBY.** *"They killed my son."*

**LIANE.** Where is Jordan? Jordan?

> *(She tries to get up.* **TOBY** *hops up to catch her before she falls to the floor, she goes floppy in* **TOBY***'s arms.)*

Where is Jordan?

**TOBY.** He just stepped out for a sec. (Can you –)

> *(He looks to* **REGGIE** *for help with* **LIANE***.)*

**REGGIE.** Oh, um...

> *(***REGGIE** *does that thing with her hands where she's in a kind of posture of helping but not actually doing anything.)*

**TOBY.** Uh, I got it.

**LIANE.** (I cheated on him.)

**TOBY.** Oh!

**LIANE.** YEP.

**TOBY.** You don't need to...

**LIANE.** Soorrrry.

**TOBY.** That's okay.

**LIANE.** He sends me treats to my work on our anniversary. He likes to make a BIG SHOW OF IT.

**TOBY.**  Oh, that is a type.

**LIANE.**  He has sixteen. Instagram followers. He's too old to have an Instagram. I don't have one, my third graders have them. I don't want my students to see the kind of food I eat.

**TOBY.**  No, that would be strange.

**LIANE.**  He likes to post pictures of me when I flatiron my hair.

**TOBY.**  Hm.

**LIANE.**  His stubble feels like toast.

**TOBY.**  That's no good.

**LIANE.**  I wonder if he sends treats to work so when we get DIVORCED. My friends will take his side. Like… "But those amazing doughnuts. They had pistachios on them. And real fruit. My husband only ever sent me… a balloon."

**TOBY.**  He's here with you!

**LIANE.**  Where is he? Where is my hair?

**TOBY.**  Why don't you rest for a bit? Lie back.

**LIANE.**  You have a good spirit. You're like…a daffodil. With big muscular arms.

**TOBY.**  Th-thank you.

**LIANE.**  I thought there would be orchids. Moth orchids. Like the website…I think they used stock images… I never should have left Ohio. I don't know why Jordan thinks something in New York City is better than something anywhere else. He fucking hates himself.

## (1 P.M.)

(**LIANE** *is asleep in* **JORDAN**'s *lap. It's one p.m.* **DENISE** *comes out with* **CLYDE**. *They are both laughing.)*

**CLYDE**.  That's what I said to him. Don't tell me about sharks, I married one.

(**DENISE** *laughs even harder.)*

**DENISE**.  Oh, Clyde.

(**CLYDE** *chuckles, sits and grabs his crossword puzzle.* **DENISE** *pulls herself together.)*

Reggie?

**REGGIE**.  Yeah?

(**DENISE** *crouches to get on* **REGGIE**'s *seated level.)*

**DENISE**.  I'm letting you know that... Your last slide came back clear. Okay? We got a really nice margin. As far as these go, this was a *very* friendly tumor. No nasty roots. Okay? It's all gone.

(**DENISE** *waits for a response.* **REGGIE** *is surprised and embarrassed to find herself suddenly sobbing.* **DENISE** *is smiling at* **REGGIE**, *hands her a tissue from one of those little tissue packs she keeps in her scrubs.)*

Hey! Hey there! It's good news!

(**DENISE** *comforts her.)*

**REGGIE**.  Yeah I know. I don't think I was letting myself... Feel very much about all this?

**DENISE**.  I hope you feel happy now.

**REGGIE.**  No offense but I didn't want my nose to look like Clyde's.

**CLYDE.**  What, you don't like rutabagas?

> (**REGGIE** *blows her nose as best she can with her bandage.*)

**DENISE.**  That was not my work. That was before my time.

**REGGIE.**  So what happens now?

> (**DENISE** *produces a medical model head.*)

**DENISE.**  Well, you're cancer free. So. All we have to do is close up that hole! We do have a special way of closing up this kind of hole. Because it's on your nose, and because the defect is about the size of a dime, we're going to make a skin graft with a piece of your forehead. But we want to keep some blood flow through the graft so that it heals really nicely. The way we do that is we cut two incisions. In your forehead. We pull the flap of skin down. We twist the skin around. It stays connected to your forehead, so we keep that blood flow. We sew the tip of the flap onto the hole on your nose, close the incision in the forehead, and then in three weeks you come back here, and we'll disconnect your forehead from your nose.

**REGGIE.**  ... ... ...What?

**DENISE.**  Mhm!

**REGGIE.**  I don't want that!

**DENISE.**  We do this all the time.

**REGGIE.**  I don't want that.

**DENISE.**  It blends in with the nose, and you can cover the forehead scar.

**REGGIE.**  NO. I don't want this.

**DENISE.**  I know it seems scary... But we *are* going to do this.

REGGIE. Is this why you wanted me to talk to a psychiatrist? Because if I look at myself in the mirror like that I'm gonna go batshit crazy?

DENISE. If you need that support, we can arrange it for you.

REGGIE. I want my Healthcare Proxy.

DENISE. And who is that?

REGGIE. My sister. She's not here and I want to talk to her before you do that.

DENISE. Okay, is your sister a doctor?

REGGIE. No, but she has excellent judgment.

DENISE. She's not going to be able to tell you more than I am.

REGGIE. I need her help. And you will NOT be doing this "flap" until I consult with her.

DENISE. It's gonna be a better outcome the fresher this wound is.

REGGIE. A few hours? Please?

DENISE. I can't advise you to wait on this.

REGGIE. Excuse me, but I refuse. Okay? I refuse. I need a minute.

DENISE. ...All right. You need a minute. That's okay.

(**CLYDE** *chuckles.*)

CLYDE. Hey good for you, kid.

REGGIE. What?

CLYDE. You're home free!

REGGIE. Oh...yeah.

CLYDE. Must feel good?

(**REGGIE** *goes a little cloudy.*)

**REGGIE.**  ...Is it bad that I'm more worried about how it'll look than not having cancer anymore?

**CLYDE.**  ... ... ...Nah. When I had this hunk of meat clipped out, I was in the dumps for weeks.

**REGGIE.**  Do you think I did the right thing?

**CLYDE.**  *(Chuckling.)* What? Telling the doctor to buzz off?

**REGGIE.**  Yeah!

**CLYDE.**  No one does it! I never do that. I'm like a baby in here. They tell me to do anything and I do it.

**REGGIE.**  It just didn't feel right to me.

>  (**REGGIE** *goes to get a snack from the vending machine.* **TOBY** *and* **PAULA** *enter with meatball subs in a bag.)*

**TOBY.**  I mean, I've been putting everything off since Lindsey was born, I've had this giant pile of laundry that keeps growing and it's, at this point, leaning to the side? And I keep cleaning the top part of it? But I swear to god the bottom of the pile has not been cleaned since the summer I don't even know what's down there.

There's an orange on the counter that looks like a walnut at this point. And the thing is, I have so many moles. I have a mole on the other nipple, they look exactly the same to me. I don't even totally believe that one of them is cancer and the other isn't? It's just like, such an *annoying* thing to deal with. So I put it off and put it off blah blah blah.

**PAULA.**  Is work going okay at least?

**TOBY.**  *(Smiling.)* I mean no.

**PAULA.**  I thought you liked it?

**TOBY.**  *(Laughing.)* I assure you I have never said that.

**PAULA.**  I'm sorry I don't really know what it *is* you do.

**TOBY.** *(Not even sure himself.)* I mean... It's marketing?

**PAULA.** What *is* that?

**TOBY.** It's basically writing...little internet lists.

**PAULA.** Why don't you send them to me?

**TOBY.** Because I'm a corporate shill. I thought when I got into it that it was like, eco-friendly. But turns out that's like how arborists all work in the logging industry.

**PAULA.** I've been telling Bebbie and Joan you're an environmental journalist.

**TOBY.** Let Bebbie and Joan think that.

**PAULA.** Bebbie was impressed. You know / Ben is working for ProPublica now?

**TOBY.** I know I saw about Ben.

**PAULA.** Last time / you were here –

**TOBY.** *(Amused.)* They don't put me on clients like that anymore. No, they gave me an assignment a while back on this embalming fluid manufacturer?

**PAULA.** Oh, ew.

**TOBY.** It leaks out of caskets and into the groundwater, and I had to say, "And that's a good thing!" It's terrible. I think of Lindsey, how many ancestors she'll grow up drinking.

**PAULA.** She's with Terry?

**TOBY.** Terry went back to work. Lindsey's at day care.

**PAULA.** Why didn't you leave her with me?

**TOBY.** *(Good-natured.)* I don't want you taking her to some...pediatric chiropractor.

**PAULA.** You loved Sunseed!

**TOBY.** *(He did love Sunseed, but.)* She didn't know I had scoliosis.

**PAULA.**  That is just a label.

**TOBY.**  Why did I need an adjustment when I was two hours old?

**PAULA.**  Oh, pooh. Let me babysit!

**TOBY.**  *(Sweet.)* But, Mom, I wanted you to be here with *me* today.

**PAULA.**  *Really?* I guess I thought skin cancer was not a big deal? You know Bebbie had skin cancer?

**TOBY.**  I'm sorry to hear that.

**PAULA.**  She didn't see a doctor. She didn't have it cut off.

She got this salve from Australia and she just cared for it, and the whole thing sloughed right off. Have you looked into that?

**TOBY.**  *(Patient and smiling.)* My nipple –

**PAULA.**  SHHH! Shhh...

**TOBY.**  – is in a trash can, so, if you want to fish it out and put it back on, and get me this cream from Austria?

**PAULA.**  Australia.

**TOBY.**  Be my guest.

**PAULA.**  But don't let them just sew you up, the thread has toxins. Every toxin you put in your body, you *have* to *purge.*

**TOBY.**  That's what kidneys do.

**PAULA.**  You have to *help them.*

**TOBY.**  *(Nodding and smiling.)* You are eating a meatball.

**PAULA.**  I purge my toxins.

**REGGIE.**  Hey uh so...cancer is a toxin that gets into your bloodstream.

**PAULA.** *(Earth mother.)* … …Thank you. Thank you for that. Good luck with everything… Toby, honey, honey! The finest doctor we have is our own body. Does it hurt?

**TOBY.** *(Poking the bandage.)* It's numb.

**PAULA.** I should get you in to see my new woman. Doctor Teresa, on Lex, by Gina's old place.

**TOBY.** What happened to Sunseed?

**PAULA.** Oh honey! Sunseed died!

**TOBY.** *(Sweet.)* Aw, I'm sorry, Ma.

**PAULA.** Doctor Teresa is not *just* a chiropractor, she does *everything*. She will change your *life*.

**TOBY.** *(Genuinely appreciative.)* I appreciate that you're trying to help, but I've found a plan, and I just need you to keep me company.

> **(PAULA** *stares at him unblinking, waits a second, and continues.)*

**PAULA.** She takes your clothes off and then she puts you in these high clogs on a table, and she knocks different body parts together.

Christian Slater used to see her! Or, she has a picture of him on her wall, so I assume. Was the sandwich okay?

**TOBY.** It was great. I've been trying to eat less meat. But. Whatever.

**PAULA.** Why?

**TOBY.** *(Goofy voice.)* Just the old depression, peekin' on through. (I still take Wellbutrin.)

**PAULA.** You shouldn't do that.

**TOBY.** *(Oops!)* I know.

**PAULA.** Aminoketones are *not good* for your brain chemistry. Long term? Your brain needs to learn how to go it alone.

**TOBY**.  *(Optimistic.)* It was helping for a while.

**PAULA**.  But that's just it. It works for a while and then, the brain craves more.

**TOBY**.  I saw this article about a starving whale that got stuck in a canal? And, I was like, yes! That...That is me.

**PAULA**.  Oh, Toby.

**TOBY**.  Like my blowhole is so close to the surface, but I can't get air, so I'm breathing in water. And I have to eat so many tiny krill and it's never enough, and there's nowhere to go. I read somewhere eating meat makes it worse but I keep craving shrimp cocktail. And now I'm like... Why did I even come here, did I not have to come here?

**PAULA**.  You didn't have to. Hospitals don't think of you as an actual person. This is why finding a holistic doctor is so important, to cut off this cycle.

**TOBY**.  *(Smiling.)* This whole thing has felt so.

**PAULA**.  Trauma.

**TOBY**.  *(Laughing.)* Bad!

**PAULA**.  It's trauma.

**TOBY**.  *(Optimistic.)* You know when you go to a restaurant, and ask the server for a recommendation, and they give you a bunch, but none of them sound good? So you just do something else? That's how I feel. I want something else.

**PAULA**.  You don't need doctors. You can heal yourself.

**TOBY**.  *(Really asking.)* How?

**PAULA**.  It is impossible for the body to heal when you are in survival mode. The gut holds on to everything, hoarding anything it might need, every fear that you need to let go of lingers. You need to integrate holistic modalities that will initiate a cascade of healing.

Sound organizes matter, changes the geometry of water, can exert a physical force strong enough to levitate a droplet of water, the body is made up of water, what are the sounds you're immersed in? Cultivate compassionate presence, contemplative care, the biology of belief. Essential oils. Diffuse them into the air. (You have to get a diffuser that vibrates the atoms so that your body can absorb the energy, you can buy it from me directly, you get a discount and I get a commission so everyone wins.) Stress. Stress kills. You work long hours, you don't have a mantra, it makes the body sick. That cycle of negative thinking can reprogram your cells, it can make your cells go: "Oh… I'm not wanted in this body. There is a war in this body and I'm going to rebel. I'm taking a stand against this body that refuses to care for me and so I am spreading and growing and I will not be stopped." Your thoughts are killing your skin. It's / dying.

CLYDE.   WHAT THE HELL ARE YOU TALKING ABOUT?? I mean really, what in god's name are you referring to?

PAULA.  Excuse me, I am having a private conversation with my son? Who is currently in treatment for cancer.

CLYDE.  And what the hell am I?

PAULA.  You have a lot of anger and I suggest you back off.

CLYDE.  I'm asking you an honest question.

PAULA.  It feels extremely disingenuous, actually.

CLYDE.  I'll put it to you this way: what you just said…

PAULA.  …Yes.

CLYDE.  About…

PAULA.  Are you expecting me to ask your question for you?

CLYDE.  I don't want to put words in your mouth!

**PAULA.** Then don't!

**CLYDE.** You implied to your son... What, what you're implying is, it's, it's appalling!

**PAULA.** "Appalling" – who are you?

**CLYDE.** You're saying this is his fault.

**PAULA.** Not fault but, we get out what we put in.

**CLYDE.** Health is not a natural state! The moment life begins, it starts to decay.

**PAULA.** I wouldn't know anything about that, sir.

**REGGIE.** You said he was to blame for his skin dying. You're blaming him for having skin! Skin dies. That's what it does!

**PAULA.** There are ways.

**LIANE.** What are you talking about?

**PAULA.** You can program your cells to grow better and longer.

**REGGIE.** How? How do you do that?

**PAULA.** You have no idea. You have no idea what... The sun? Gives us energy.

If you take the energy from the sun? And you turn it into cancer? You are doing it wrong! You are doing it way wrong!

**JORDAN.** I mean she's right. About the sun. Sunlight, and cholesterol in skin, and – that's what you mean?

**PAULA.** Absolutely not.

**JORDAN.** Okay, you know what? I really shouldn't have butted in here.

**REGGIE.** I want to hear.

**JORDAN.** I don't want to get involved.

**PAULA.** If you have cancer, something you did caused it.

**REGGIE.** *Jesus Christ!*

**CLYDE.** This is genetic. It's inherited.

**PAULA.** We don't inherit anything.

**TOBY.** *(Ever so sweetly.)* Mama?

**PAULA.** What?

**TOBY.** *(Asking for a favor.)* Can you be a little more respectful to these people?

**PAULA.** You don't even know them.

**TOBY.** *(So gently.)* No but, I get what they're saying. I feel like you're blaming me.

**PAULA.** Oh, honey, I'm not blaming you. Is that what you think?

**REGGIE.** That's completely what you're doing.

**TOBY.** *(Confused.)* Can you mind your business?

**REGGIE.** Me?

**TOBY.** I didn't say anything when you were going on about Hamas this morning.

**REGGIE.** I was…I was not going on about Hamas! I don't even know what Hamas is necessarily!

**PAULA.** Let us not gang up on this innocent child.

**REGGIE.** I'm nineteen!

**TOBY.** *(Gently curious.)* Where are the doctors? Why is no one in there?

**CLYDE.** They're having lunch. They have to eat.

**PAULA.** I'm sure some pharmaceutical reps took them out.

**REGGIE.** Do you think?

**CLYDE.** Oh come on… You can't have this kind of mentality.

**PAULA**. And what mentality is that?

**CLYDE**. Oh! Everyone's out to get you! At a certain point, you have to trust people.

**PAULA**. I have no reason to do that.

**CLYDE**. I do, this woman has been treating me for years. I have respect for her.

**PAULA**. They keep you coming back.

**CLYDE**. It's a disease. They can't help that I'm like this. They just treat it when it comes up!

**PAULA**. They keep you sick with language. You're only sick because that's the language they have given you.

**CLYDE**. What kind of thing is that to say? You think the way something is described has any impact on reality?

**PAULA**. Of course it does.

**CLYDE**. You are out of your gourd, lady.

**PAULA**. Snake oil salesman...

**CLYDE**. YOU'RE THE SNAKE OIL SALESMAN, MA'AM!

**REGGIE**. Can you guys stop?

**CLYDE**. I apologize. This is not uh, appropriate behavior.

**PAULA**. I'm not the one yelling.

**CLYDE**. I'm just trying to get my point across.

**PAULA**. In the first World War, you know how they treated shell shock? Food. Comfort. Rest. And almost all of them got better. But you can't put a patent on that.

**CLYDE**. You know, in the eighties –

**PAULA**. What are you saying now?

**CLYDE**. *(Thundering.)* LET ME SPEAK. In the eighties. There was this guy. Street artist. Richard Hambleton. Hung out in the Village, ya know, quiet nice guy. He made these silhouettes of a man. "The Shadowman." You'd see one around a corner and it'd give you a chill. They were freaky. Scorched into brick. And Richard, he had...terrible, terrible skin cancer. He was ravaged by it. And he was determined not to get treatment. He was living with a bunch of young arty kids, and they had convinced him that if he just thought positive! It would go away. Do you know what happens if you don't get this taken care of? I used to see him gettin' coffee at St. Dymphna's, and every time I saw him, there was less and less of him. His lips, his cheeks, his nose went necrotic. His eye sockets peeling away from the bone. He was turning into a skull, and then it wrapped around his optic nerve and rooted into his brain, and he died. So. Don't go telling this kid. Who you love. Don't tell him he doesn't need a doctor.

**TOBY.** I've only been in there once.

**CLYDE.** Really?

**JORDAN.** That's strange.

  (**JONATHAN** *steps out, looking at his laptop.*)

**LIANE.** I've been in a lot.

**TOBY.** *(Shrugging.)* Just once.

**PAULA.** Maybe they forgot about you.

**TOBY.** *(To* **JONATHAN.***)* Sorry, do you know if I can go?

**JONATHAN.** We don't have any news for you yet. I'll personally let you know the minute we hear back. Liane?

**LIANE.** *Again?*

  (**LIANE** *goes back with* **JONATHAN. JORDAN** *tries to get pretzels from the machine. They almost come out but they're suspended, and won't drop. He bumps and shakes the machine until they drop.* **JONATHAN** *returns.)*

**JONATHAN.** Jordan, would you mind coming with me?

**JORDAN.** Why?

**JONATHAN.** I just need you to follow me in.

**JORDAN.** I don't understand.

**JONATHAN.** Your wife wants to talk to you.

**JORDAN.** She goes in. I don't go in. I stay out here, and she goes in.

**JONATHAN.** She wants you to come and see her.

**JORDAN.** I don't want to see.

**JONATHAN.** She'd like to talk to you about what's going on. About the plan for today. You may need to make some arrangements.

**JORDAN.** I can't.

(**JORDAN** *sits down and belligerently eats his pretzels.* **JONATHAN** *goes.)*

**PAULA.** What's that all about?

**REGGIE.** Sh!

(**JONATHAN** *returns with* **DENISE.***)*

**DENISE.** Jordan? We'd like to speak with you in the room with your wife.

**JORDAN.** I already told the kid, I'm not going.

**DENISE.** Alright. We've been as conservative as possible, we're deep in her orbit and we're not finding the root of this thing.

The MRI results indicate that the sarcoma is fixed to the skull at the back of the orbit. Further radiation is not going to address this, she'll need to have the eye removed. She's elected to proceed with the surgery here, today. So what's going to happen is we'll take her upstairs for general surgery, and we'll bring her back here afterwards. You'll be able to do all the necessary wound care at home, in the comfort of your own space. Do you have any questions?

*(A very long pause.)*

**JORDAN.** You said you were going to rule it out?

**DENISE.** Right, we had talked about this possibility.

**JORDAN.** But "rule it out," you couldn't rule it out?

**DENISE.** No.

**JORDAN.** Why do I have to take her home? Can't you keep her here?

**JONATHAN.** This is an outpatient facility. We don't "keep" people.

**JORDAN.** Can you make an exception?

**DENISE.** It's not necessary, so even if we were to transfer her to inpatient your insurance wouldn't cover it.

**JORDAN.** She drove. She drove us here. I um. I have my hand I can't.

**JONATHAN.** You'll have to get a cab or something.

**JORDAN.** We don't live here. The car is parked on the street. Can...do we...leave it or?

**(JONATHAN** *looks to* **DENISE** *for what to do.)*

**DENISE.** You'll have to make arrangements.

**JORDAN.** What will she look like?

**DENISE.** ...We'll take the graft from skin on her hip and thigh. So, it'll be a patch of skin. Like...a thigh.

*(Pause.)*

JORDAN.  Could you just – not do this? Is there a way – not to?

DENISE.  I'm sorry.

JORDAN.  What if I refuse? That girl refused.

DENISE.  Your wife has elected to go ahead with it today.

JORDAN.  Don't I have a say in this?

DENISE.  ?! No.

JONATHAN.  ...Would you like to speak with Liane? I know she would like to see you, before.

JORDAN.  I'm sorry.

DENISE.  Alright.

*(The doctors go.)*

*(Everyone is trying not to look at* **JORDAN**, *but everyone is looking at* **JORDAN**. **JORDAN** *packs up his things, and starts to leave.)*

REGGIE.  Where are you going?

JORDAN.  I'll be right back.

REGGIE.  *Where are you going?*

JORDAN.  I'll be right back.

(**JORDAN** *leaves. A cloudy pause.* **PAULA** *pulls an enormous crystal singing bowl out of her bag.)*

PAULA.  Sweetie, I –

TOBY.  *(Almost laughing.)* No.

PAULA.  *(Announcing.)* I brought my bowls.

TOBY.  Mom...

PAULA.  I'll infuse it with reiki so everyone will benefit.

*(**CLYDE** rolls his eyes. **PAULA** plays her bowls by running her mallet around the rims, everyone receives the reiki through its resonance. It's good stuff. It should wash over the audience so everyone feels it.)*

*(**JONATHAN** enters.)*

**JONATHAN.** Toby?

## (3 P.M.)

(**TOBY** *stands and packs his bag up.*)

**CLYDE.**  It doesn't make sense.

**TOBY.**  I can go home.

**CLYDE.**  I've never heard of such a thing.

**TOBY.**  I'm extremely relieved.

**CLYDE.**  They only did one pass.

**TOBY.**  They couldn't find *anything*. "Spontaneous remission."

>   (**CLYDE** *searches around the room for anyone's help.*)

**CLYDE.**  The whole point of this is that there weren't clear margins on the biopsy. I don't understand how the first pass could be totally clear. Clear margins, sure, but totally clear?

**TOBY.**  You said to trust them. You said *you* trust them.

**CLYDE.**  Of course I do, but I know how this goes.

**PAULA.**  Will you leave my son alone, please?

**CLYDE.**  I'm expressing concern, I'm concerned about you.

**PAULA.**  We appreciate that, we've really appreciated all of your concern today, sir.

**TOBY.**  I haven't felt this good in months. I'm gonna eat clean, I'm gonna meditate. I'm gonna start going to church again.

**PAULA.**  Will you, Toby? That would make me so happy.

>   (**TOBY** *and* **PAULA** *leave.*)

**CLYDE.**  Maybe I can talk to the doctors about it.

**REGGIE.** No you can't. You can't talk with the doctors about some random man's medical information.

**CLYDE.** That doesn't seem strange to you?

**REGGIE.** That he came in for treatment and left, cancer free? No it's not.

**CLYDE.** If they didn't find anything, they didn't need to bring him here in the first place.

**REGGIE.** Maybe they got it all the first time, but couldn't tell.

**CLYDE.** I'm not some contrarian, you have to understand.

**REGGIE.** He's healthy. Be happy for him.

**CLYDE.** That's not what this is about!

**REGGIE.** Miracles happen.

**CLYDE.** Don't you ever get worried about someone?

**REGGIE.** Of course.

**CLYDE.** I'm worried.

**REGGIE.** You really think you know more than the doctors do?

**CLYDE.** They aren't perfect.

**REGGIE.** You're the one who said he shouldn't doubt them.

**CLYDE.** I think people should trust their doctor. But, you know, keep your eyes open, ask questions. It's a collaboration. What happened to that man doesn't make sense. He should get a second opinion!

**REGGIE.** Then go. Go after him. Tell him that!

(**CLYDE** *nods. Then he thinks.*)

**CLYDE.** He's probably fine.

# (4 P.M.)

(**CLYDE** *packs up his stuff.*)

**REGGIE.**  Good for you.

**CLYDE.**  Yeah. Good for me.

(**CLYDE** *leaves.*)

## (5 P.M.)

**ANNA.** Just do it, Reggie.

**REGGIE.** Are you seeing this?

**JONATHAN.** We should be heading into the room now.

**ANNA.** You can't just leave it open. They have to close it up. So go close it up!

**JONATHAN.** I know it looks scary but it's really kind of amazing.

**REGGIE.** I'd have to be like that for three weeks. My forehead cut open, skin dangling down, I'm supposed to walk around like that?

**JONATHAN.** Some people do.

**REGGIE.** How do I go to class like that?

**ANNA.** Do it, and let's go home.

**REGGIE.** I don't want my forehead on my nose!

**ANNA.** How else are they going to do it?

**REGGIE.** Honestly any other way!

**JONATHAN.** You are the last patient.

**ANNA.** Go.

(**REGGIE** *sits.*)

**REGGIE.** Maybe I can just...care for it? Maybe I can just eat clean and it will heal?

**JONATHAN.** The problem is that your skin has been removed, and it's not going to grow back.

(**REGGIE** *looks to* **ANNA** *for help.*)

**ANNA.** I know it sounds super messed up. I get it, I wouldn't want to do this either. But you made a choice to do this. You have to go back in, and get your head closed shut.

**JONATHAN**. Your sister is right.

(**DENISE** *enters*.)

**DENISE**. Hi, Reggie. What's going on?

**REGGIE**. I don't want this horrible twisty thing.

**DENISE**. Long term, you're going to be happier. When you're forty –

**REGGIE**. Who cares what I'll look like when I'm forty!

**DENISE & ANNA**. You will.

**REGGIE**. I'm gonna look like a monster!

**DENISE**. It's only three weeks.

**REGGIE**. That's forever!

**ANNA**. No it's not!

This is not a real problem, what is the problem here?

**REGGIE**. What if the flap gets caught on a rusty nail?

**ANNA**. What?

**REGGIE**. What, what if the flap gets caught and it's like the hangnail in *Black Swan* but with my forehead!

**DENISE**. You will need to be careful with it.

**REGGIE**. What if it doesn't work? Is it possible it just won't work?

**DENISE**. There's a very small chance the graft would fail.

**REGGIE**. Fail!

**DENISE**. It's a teeny tiny chance.

**REGGIE**. What do you mean fail!?

**DENISE**. The flap would...die.

**REGGIE**. THE FLAP WOULD DIE!? ANNA!

**ANNA**. It's a small chance!

**REGGIE.** I just want a regular scar! I don't want some crazy scar!

**ANNA.** I know what it's like to have a crazy scar, I have a scar from my neck to my stomach, dumbass – remember when I was BORN WITHOUT A FUNCTIONING AORTA?

**REGGIE.** It's not on your face.

**ANNA.** It's my bikini face, and it's not a big deal. It looks a little scary, okay? But the only people who care are the worst people in the world. Like if I take off my shirt, and a guy's like. "What is that?" I'm like, "Bye. What's for lunch?"

**REGGIE.** It's going to look scary!

**ANNA.** Oh honey... Honey! They can do anything.

**REGGIE.** They can't. I've seen what they do. It always looks messed up.

And my personality is already so abrasive, Anna, I don't think I can pull off being gay, pretentious, and disfigured.

**ANNA.** Forget I said that!

**REGGIE.** How will someone ever fall in love with me if I don't have a face?

**ANNA.** You're going to have *a face*.

**REGGIE.** Anna. I just want a regular-ass scar. It's just what I want.

> *(This makes sense to **ANNA**. **ANNA** goes into Finance Mode.)*

**ANNA.** Okay listen, Doc. We want a regular-ass scar over here. What is it gonna take to get it?

**JONATHAN.** This isn't...the wild west. We can't just make it happen.

**ANNA**. This sounds like a pretty sophisticated operation. Any chance Young Sheldon over here just wants to get some practice in at the expense of my sister's face?

**JONATHAN**. Absolutely not.     **DENISE**. No.

**ANNA**. Well that's what it sounds like to me. And I see you have a plush little deal over here with your reps.

      (**JONATHAN** *rolls his eyes.*)

**DENISE**. *(Exasperated.) It's a cancer medication.* The funds go to our care staff. We don't benefit from it.

**ANNA**. *(Assured but still pissed off.)*...That's nice. That's nice of you.

**DENISE**. This is going to be a good surgical solution.

**ANNA**. You're gonna find another way to do this or we're gonna have a problem. I'll take her somewhere else.

**DENISE**. No. She needs to have this closed today. Reggie, you are mid-surgery. I know that seems strange because you're awake and walking around, but we're not done here.

**REGGIE**. I came in today with a face. I know I'll get more of these, and I know someday a day will come where I really am screwed and you'll really have to make me unrecognizable, but I'm not ready for that yet. I want my face. I need a few more years with my face.

**DENISE**. ...We can try a straight closure. It's not going to look as good as a graft. But if you know that? And you agree to that? We can do it.

**ANNA**. Is that okay with you?

**REGGIE**. That's what I want.

**ANNA**. Okay. Okay. We have a deal.

## (7 P.M.)

(**LIANE** *sits alone, her eyes fully bandaged. Drains connected to fluid collection bulbs peek out from the bandaging, her leg is in a graft cast.* **ANNA** *and* **REGGIE** *walk in from the surgical suite.* **JONATHAN** *is looking at* **LIANE.**)

**LIANE**. Jordan?

(**LIANE** *reaches over to the chair next to her, feels the seat.*)

Jordan?

**JONATHAN**. Um. Do you know where her, uh, husband is?

(**REGGIE** *shakes her head.*)

Someone needs to sign her out.

**LIANE**. Where is Jordan?

**REGGIE**. He's not here.

**LIANE**. When? When did he leave?

**REGGIE**. Five? Six hours ago? Can you call him?

(**LIANE** *shakes her head, "No no no!"*)

**ANNA**. Do you have a place to stay?

(**LIANE** *shakes her head.*)

We can help you get a hotel room?

**LIANE**. Can I stay with you?

**ANNA**. With me?

**LIANE**. With you two.

**ANNA**. I...I live in a studio apartment with my bulldog and one chair. I also... I don't know you.

(*Pause.*)

**REGGIE**.  Alcove.

**ANNA**.  What?

**REGGIE**.  It's an alcove studio.

**ANNA**.  I'm not a hospital! I set up an air mattress for you to stay on.

**REGGIE**.  We can snuggle up!

**ANNA**.  With your nose like that?

**REGGIE**.  We'll figure it out.

**ANNA**.  I don't know how to take care of her.

**REGGIE**.  Anna. You need to do this. You need to do this for me.

(*Pause.*)

**ANNA**.  (*Without looking at* **LIANE**.) What kind of food do you like to eat, Liane?

**LIANE**.  Cottage cheese with pineapple. And um, Toblerones.

**ANNA**.  We can get you those.

**LIANE**.  Okay.

**REGGIE**.  Okay.

(**ANNA** *signs* **LIANE** *out.* **JONATHAN** *goes.*)

**ANNA**.  I live in a walk-up. They didn't give you a cane or anything?

(**LIANE** *makes a single abrupt sob.*)

Hey. It's gonna be okay. They can do – amazing things these days. They *made Cher*. So.

We're gonna take you home. Okay? You're coming home with us.

## (8 P.M.)

*(After work, **JONATHAN** is alone in the waiting room, charting on a laptop. **DENISE** comes on, also charting on a laptop.)*

**JONATHAN**. Thank you so much for asking to chat with me! Want one?

*(**JONATHAN** offers her a beer.)*

**DENISE**. Oh, no, thanks.

*(**DENISE** looks at the cardboard woman.)*

Hey, let's toss this?

*(Pause.)*

**JONATHAN**. Really?

*(Little pause.)*

**DENISE**. Yyeah...

*(Pause.)*

**JONATHAN**. The rep is coming next week.

*(Little pause.)*

**DENISE**. It's just not worth it.

*(Pause.)*

**JONATHAN**. What about Patty?

*(Little pause.)*

**DENISE**. I'll tell her.

*(Pause.)*

**JONATHAN**. Okay.

> (**JONATHAN** *takes the cardboard cutout out, comes back.* **DENISE** *is steeling herself.*)

Do you not drink?

**DENISE**. Not really anymore. Sometimes on birthdays.

**JONATHAN**. I think it's a nice way of marking the end of the day. To tell myself, "You're done!" "You can relax!"

**DENISE**. I feel that way about lunch.

**JONATHAN**. Yeah?

**DENISE**. I like to have a little piece of chocolate after lunch to tell myself... Lunch is done... I'm sorry you missed your show.

**JONATHAN**. All day I was like, "Oh man... This day is brutal. At least at the end of it, I get to see *Waitress.*" ...

> (*Pause.*)

I thought I would see so many musicals when I got to New York... But, where is the time?

> (*Pause.*)

**DENISE**. When I matched here I thought I would go surfing all the time.

> (*Pause.*)

(*Ominous.*) No one understands that New York is a beach town.

**JONATHAN**. ...Can I ask you something?

**DENISE**. Alright.

**JONATHAN**. How did you find your way? Into this specialty?

**DENISE**. Oh.

(**DENISE** *thinks about whether she wants to get into this now or not. Then proceeds, gently, confessing.*)

Well I always liked derm. But I had this idea that it wasn't a serious enough specialty. So I did emergency for a year.

**JONATHAN.** Really?

**DENISE.** Oh yeah.

**JONATHAN.** What happened?

**DENISE.** 9/11.

**JONATHAN.** *(Excited.)* Oh! What was that like?

**DENISE.** *(Like it's nothing.)* I mean... We were outside Bellevue with stretchers all day. No one came. I felt useless. And I thought, screw it. Why not do the thing I actually like? So I went back and did it all again. What about you?

**JONATHAN.** My dad. Melanoma.

**DENISE.** Oh I see.

**JONATHAN.** He passed when I was in high school.

**DENISE.** I'm sorry to hear that.

**JONATHAN.** Oh, thanks.

(*Pause.*)

**DENISE.** But that's not the only reason you're doing this?

**JONATHAN.** That's what's kept me going.

**DENISE.** But you have a passion for it!

**JONATHAN.** Well yeah, I wanted to do surgery because I figured I wouldn't have to interact with patients that much!

**DENISE.** Medicine is social. You can't get away from that.

**JONATHAN.**  I've never not been in school. I feel like I've forgotten how to talk to people.

    *(Pause.)*

**DENISE.**  Are you sure this is the right path for you?

**JONATHAN.**  *(Laughing.)* I'm half a million in debt, it better be!

**DENISE.**  You could go into research?

**JONATHAN.**  Whoa whoa whoa!

**DENISE.**  Do you want to be here?

**JONATHAN.**  I'm sorry if I've given you the impression I'm not enthusiastic. I really haven't gotten a chance yet to tell you how grateful I am. To be here? In this town? Learning from you?

This is the hardest thing I've ever done and I feel so grateful... Is this what you wanted to talk to me about?

**DENISE.**  *(Gently.)* I asked you to chat because – you made a mistake today. The lab couldn't find a malignancy on that patient's first slide because you excised the wrong side.

    *(Pause.)*

**JONATHAN.**  There was nothing on the entire slide! That's the best possible outcome.

**DENISE.**  Finding nothing on an area where there was something means you missed the spot entirely.

**JONATHAN.**  Spontaneous remission!

**DENISE.**  You did the wrong side.

**JONATHAN.**  You don't know that. How can you say that? You don't know that!

**DENISE.**  You didn't write which side you excised in your note, so how can you be sure?

**JONATHAN.** Because I did whichever side the previous note said!

**DENISE.** And what side was that?

**JONATHAN.** That's such a rookie mistake I wouldn't have done that!

**DENISE.** Wanna bet his life on it?

**JONATHAN.** I asked him, "Is this correct?" He said, "Yes." I wrote my initials on his skin.

**DENISE.** People forget. He was on the table with a pre-melanoma. He was scared.

**JONATHAN.** He was scared? I was scared! You should have been there!

**DENISE.** Excuse me?

**JONATHAN.** Why did you have to go do some bullshit insurance thing?

**DENISE.** Advocating for your patients is part of the job. If you don't like talking to them, and you don't like advocating for them, you have to ask yourself what you're doing here.

**JONATHAN.** I feel like I'm gonna throw up.

**DENISE.** I would have checked your work but you asked me to approve his discharge after you had already let him go.

**JONATHAN.** I was doing Patty's job on top of mine.

**DENISE.** You're never going to be working under ideal circumstances.

**JONATHAN.** I thought he was going to just take off.

**DENISE.** Don't let them push you.

**JONATHAN.** I am so sorry.

**DENISE.** Good. What are you going to do?

*(Pause.)*

**JONATHAN**.  Call him.

**DENISE**.  When?

**JONATHAN**.  Right now.

**DENISE**.  Okay.

> *(**JONATHAN** finds Toby's chart. His phone number.)*

> *(He puts the phone on speaker. The phone rings. Straight to voicemail. "Hi, it's Toby leave a message." Then, "The voicemail box is full. Goodbye.")*

> *(Pause.)*

When they're here, they're in your care.

**JONATHAN**.  You think he's just gone?

**DENISE**.  I don't know.

**JONATHAN**.  I can try again.

**DENISE**.  You can.

**JONATHAN**.  What if he never calls back?

**DENISE**.  Great question.

## End of Play

www.ingramcontent.com/pod-product-compliance
Lightning Source LLC
Chambersburg PA
CBHW070359120726
47909CB00008B/2917